A TEMPLAR BOOK

Devised and produced by The Templar Company plc, Pippbrook
Mill, London Road, Dorking, Surrey RH4 1JE, Great Britain.

First published in the USA by Bell Books, Boyds Mills Press Inc.,
A Highlights Company, 910 Church Street, Honesdale, PA 18431.

This edition © 1991 by The Templar Company plc

Designed by Philip Hargraves
Color separations by Positive Colour, Maldon, Essex
Printed and bound by Tien Wah Press, Singapore

Publisher Cataloging-in-Publication Data

Wood, A.J.
Beautiful birds/A.J. Wood; Illustrated by Helen Ward.
24 p.: ill.; cm.
Summary: Ten birds are boldly illustrated, each accompanied by a
simple, poetic narrative of their behavior.
ISBN: 1-878093-47-9
1. Birds-Juvenile Literature. [1. Birds.] I. Helen Ward. II. Title.
598-dc20   1991
Library of Congress Catalog Card Number: 90-085907

Helen Ward's

Beautiful Birds

with text by A.J. Wood

BELL
BOOKS

Here are the jungle birds,
high in the branches,
ready to lay some eggs
in their nests.

Here two flamingos
wade through the water,
looking for something
tasty to eat.

Here is the cockatoo,
white as a snowflake,
cleaning and preening
her beautiful feathers.

Here is a finch,
complete with a cherry,
feeding her babies who
cheep loud and long.

Here is a pelican, excellent fisherman,
standing alone with a beak full of food.

Here is the owl,
eyes full of knowing,
hooting "hello" from his
home in the tree.

Here is the toucan,
deep in the jungle,
proudly displaying his
colorful beak.

Here are two parrots,
all red and yellow,
squawking so noisily
in the treetop.

Here sit two lovebirds,
happy together,
side by side on
the branch of a tree.

And who have we here, on the back of a warthog?
Six tired bee-eaters having a rest.
Now count the other birds in this book.
Out of them all, which do you like the best?